Thomas B. Mosher , Charles Johnston

From the Upanishads

by Charles Johnston

Thomas B. Mosher , Charles Johnston

From the Upanishads
by Charles Johnston

ISBN/EAN: 9783337399443

Printed in Europe, USA, Canada, Australia, Japan

Cover: Foto ©Andreas Hilbeck / pixelio.de

More available books at **www.hansebooks.com**

FROM THE UPANISHADS

BY
CHARLES JOHNSTON

Portland, Maine
THOMAS B. MOSHER
1899

CONTENTS

FOREWORD

When the scanty shores are full
With Thought's perilous, whirling pool;
When frail Nature can no more,
Then the Spirit strikes the hour:
My servant Death, with solving rite,
Pours finite into infinite.

R. W. EMERSON.

FOREWORD.

IT is admitted, by common consent, that the works of Emerson stand at the head of American literature. The cause of their pre-eminence, it might well be added, is the rebirth, in them, of the thoughts and ideals of the most ancient Upanishads. Emerson himself was perfectly aware of this affinity; he found no fitter illustration of his understanding of immortality than the teaching of Death, with which I have begun this volume. His words may well be repeated:

"Within every man's thought is a higher thought; within the character he exhibits to-day, a higher character. The youth puts off the illusions of the child; the man puts off the ignorance and tumultuous passions of youth; proceeding thence, puts off the egotism of manhood, and becomes at last a public and universal soul. He is rising to greater heights, but also rising to realities; the other relations and circumstances dying out, he entering deeper into God, God into him, until the last garment of egotism falls, and he is with God; shares the will and immensity of the First Cause. It is curious to find the selfsame feeling, that it is not immortality but eternity, not duration but a state of abandonment to the Highest, and so the sharing of His perfection, appearing in the farthest east and west. The human mind takes no account of geography, language, or legends, but in all utters the same instinct. Yama, the lord of Death, promised Nachiketas, the son of Gautama, to grant him three boons at his own choice"—and then follows the teaching, as I have given it.

The central thought, and almost the very words of the second Upanishad here translated, concerning the worlds, and their putting forth by the Divine, are faithfully imaged in another of Emerson's essays:

"But when, following the invisible steps of thought, we come to enquire, whence is matter? and whereto? many truths arise out of the recesses of consciousness. We learn that the highest is present to the soul of man;

that the dread universal essence, which
is not wisdom, or love, or beauty, or
power, but all in one, and each en-
tirely, is that for which all things exist,
and that by which they are; that
spirit creates; that behind nature,
throughout nature, spirit is present.
As a plant upon the earth, so a man
rests upon the bosom of God; he is
nourished by unfailing fountains, and
draws, at his need, inexhaustible
power."

To cite all the passages in which
Emerson bears testimony to the truth
contained in the third passage I have
rendered: that the soul of man is one
with the immemorial Soul that wove
the worlds, would be, to repeat the
greater part of what he has written; for
this, more than anything else, is the
heart of his message. One passage,
out of many, will be enough:

"The soul gives itself, alone original and pure, to the Lonely, Original
and Pure, who, on that condition,
gladly inhabits, leads, and speaks
through it. Then it is glad, young,
and nimble. Behold, it saith, I am
born into the great, the universal mind.
I, the imperfect, adore my own per-

fect. I am somehow recipient of the
great soul, and thereby I do overlook
the sun and the stars, and feel them to
be the fair accidents and effects which
change and pass. More and more the
surges of everlasting nature enter into
me, and I become public and human
in my regards and actions. So I come
to live in thoughts, and act with ener-
gies, which are immortal."

Let me add, to these three, one
more passage, which shows the same
primeval power, that gave birth to
the imagery of ancient wisdom, once
more actively creative; a passage,
more eloquent, perhaps, than all else
that Emerson has written:

"There is no chance, and no anar-
chy, in the universe. All is system and
gradation. Every god is there, sitting
in his sphere. The young mortal
enters the hall of the firmament;
there, he is alone with them alone;
they pouring on him benedictions and
gifts, and beckoning him up to their
thrones. On the instant, and inces-
santly, fall snow-storms of illusions.
He fancies himself in a vast crowd
which sways this way and that, and
whose movements and doings he

must obey; he fancies himself poor,
orphaned, insignificant. The mad crowd drives hither and thither, now furiously commanding this thing to be done, now that. What is he that he should resist their will, and think or act for himself? Every moment new changes and new showers of deceptions to baffle and distract him. And when by and by, for an instant, the air clears, and the cloud lifts a little, there are the gods still sitting around him on their thrones; they alone, with him alone."

C. J.

TO G. W. RUSSELL

... in the flowers & clouds
far blue hills — the soft
of November's moon ——

- never — never ——
; the heart of Man.

Ranch — Nov. 25 — California.

TO G. W. RUSSELL

THE brown and yellow of autumn are touching the chestnut-leaves again for the tenth time since those early days when we first began to seek the small old path the seers know.

On such a day as this, rejoicing in the sunlight, we lay on our backs in the grass, and, looking up into the blue, tried to think ourselves into that new world which we had suddenly discovered ourselves to inhabit. For we had caught the word, handed down with silent laughter through the ages, that we ourselves are the inventors of the game of life, the kings of this most excellent universe: that there is no sorrow, but fancy weaves it; that we need not even knock to be admitted, for we already are, and always were, though we had forgotten it, within the doors of life.

That young enthusiasm and hourly joy of living was one of old destiny's gracious presents, a brightness to

To
G. W. Russell

remember when storms gathered round us, as they did many a time in the years since: there was a gaiety and lightness in the air then, a delight of new discovery, that I do not think we shall find again; yet I know, and you also know, what excellent strength we have gained instead. For, carrying our high hopes with us, all these years, as one side of life after another was turned to us, as we had to pass through rough ways as well as smooth, to wrestle with the stubborn tendencies of things, full-breasted and strenuous, we have fought and worked into ourselves an intimate knowledge of what we then only divined, we have realized much that then loomed dim and ghostly before us, we have learned to abide confidently by spiritual law.

To gain our experience side by side would have been very pleasant, had fate so willed it; but fate willed quite otherwise. Almost at the outset, destiny carried me, vagrant, to the distant rivers of the east, whose waters mirror old towered shrines among the palm-trees, while the boatman's song floats echo-like across; or where the breakers of the lonely, limitless ocean cast forth strange shells upon the sand; or through the grey alder-forests stretching away desolate to the frozen seas; or again, among rugged mountains, shaggy with pine-forests, where rainbow-sparkles carpet the snow.

And you, whom outward fate has held stationary, travelled perhaps further after all; finding your way homeward to the strange world the seers tell of, the world at the back of the heavens; and sending to us your "Songs by the Way."

It was an ambition of mine, in those old days, to translate, from the Indian books of Wisdom, the story of the Sacrificer's son who was sent by his father to the house of Death. This story has always seemed to me a teaching of admirable worth, carrying with it the most precious gift of all, a sense of the high mysteriousness and vast hidden treasure of life, which makes us seekers for ever, always finding, yet always knowing that there is still more to find; so that every day becomes a thing of limitless promise and wonder, only revealing itself as containing a new wonder within. For

To
G. W. Russell

what teaching could bring a more wonderful sense of the largeness and hidden riches of being than this: that our sincerest friend is the once-dreaded king of terrors; that death teaches us what no other can — the lesson of the full and present eternity of life? We need not wait till our years are closed for his teaching: that wisdom of his, like every other treasure of life, is all-present in every moment, in full abundance, here and now. It is the teaching of Death that, to gain the better, we must lose the dearer; to gain the greater, we must lose the less; to win the abundant world of reality, we must give up the world of fancy and folly and fear which we have so long held dear: we have been learning it all these years since we began; learning also Death's grim jest, that there is no sacrifice possible for us at all, for while we were painfully renouncing the dearer, his splendid generosity had already given us the better — new worlds instead of old.

Well, the ten years are passed, and my ambition is fulfilled; I hand you my rendering of Death's lesson, and

two more teachings from the same
old wise books.

I have found them wise, beyond all others; and, beyond all others, filled with that very light which makes all things new; the light discovered first within, in the secret place of the heart, and which brimming over there fills the whole of life, lightening every dark and clouded way. That glowing heart within us, we are beginning to guess, is the heart of all things, the everlasting foundation of the world; and because speech is given therein to that teaching of oneness, of our hearts and the heart eternal as eternally one, I have translated the last of these three passages from the books of Wisdom.

You will find in them, besides high intuition, a quaint and delightful flavour, a charm of childlike simplicity; yet of a child who is older than all age, a child of the eternal and infinite, whose simplicity is better than the wisdom of the wise.

There is no answer in words to the question: What is in the great Beyond? nor can there be; yet I think we know already that, in the

To
G. W. Russell
nameless mystery of the real, it will be altogether well with us — now and after. This strong reconciliation with the real is, very likely, the best fruit of our ten years' learning.

CHARLES JOHNSTON.

Ballykilbeg,
    October 15, 1895.

From the Upanishads

I

IN THE HOUSE OF DEATH

THE FIRST PART

ÂJASHRAVASA, verily, seeking favour, made a sacrifice of all he possessed. He had a son, also, by name Nachiketas. Him, though still a child, faith entered, while the gifts were being led up.

He meditated:

They have drunk water, eaten grass, given up their milk, and lost their strength. Joyless worlds, in truth, he gains, who offers these.

He addressed his father:

To whom, then, wilt thou give me? said he.

Twice and thrice he asked him.

To Death I give thee, said he.

Nachiketas ponders:

I go the first of many; I go in the midst of many. What is Death's work that he will work on me to-day?

Look, as those that have gone before, behold so are those that shall come after. As corn a mortal ripens, as corn he is born again.

Nachiketas comes to the House of Death; he speaks:

Like the Lord of Fire, a pure guest comes to the house. They offer him this greeting. Bring water, O Death, Son of the Sun!

Hope and expectation, friendship, kind words, just and holy deeds, sons and cattle, this destroys, for the foolish man in whose house a pure guest dwells without food.

After three days Death comes. Death speaks:

As thou hast dwelt three nights in my house, without food, thou, a pure guest and honourable — honour to thee, pure one, welfare to me — against this choose thou three wishes.

Nachiketas speaks:

That the descendant of Gotama may be at peace, well-minded, and with sorrow gone, towards me, O Death; that he may speak kindly to me when sent forth by thee; this, of the three, as my first wish I choose.

Death speaks:

As before will the son of Aruna, Uddâlaka's son, be kind to thee, sent forth by me; by night will he sleep well, with sorrow gone, seeing thee freed from the mouth of Death.

Nachiketas speaks:

In the heaven-world there is no fear at all; nor art thou there, nor does he fear from old age. Crossing over both hunger and thirst, and going beyond sorrow, he exults in the heaven-world.

The heavenly fire thou knowest, Death, tell it to me, for I am faithful. The heaven-worlds enjoy deathlessness; this, as my second wish, I choose.

Death speaks:

To thee I tell it; learn then from me, Nachiketas, finding the heavenly fire. Know thou also the obtaining of unending worlds, the resting-place, for this is hidden in secret.

He told him then that fire, the beginning of the worlds, and the bricks of the altar, and how many and how they are. And he again spoke it back to him as it was told; and Death, well-pleased, again addressed him.

This is thy heavenly fire, O Nachiketas, which thou hast chosen as thy second wish. This fire of thine shall they proclaim. Choose now, Nachiketas, thy third wish.

Nachiketas speaks:

This doubt that there is of a man that has gone forth: "He exists," say some; and "He exists not," others say: a knowledge of this, taught by thee, this of my wishes is the third wish.

Death speaks:

Even by the gods of old it was doubted about this; not easily knowable, and subtle is this law. Choose, Nachiketas, another wish; hold me not to it, but spare me this.

Nachiketas speaks:

Even by the gods, thou sayest, it was doubted about this; and not easily knowable is it, O Death. Another teacher of it cannot be found like thee. No other wish is equal to this.

Death speaks:

Choose sons and grandsons of a hundred years, and much cattle, and elephants and gold and horses. Choose the great abode of the earth, and for thyself live as many autumns as thou wilt.

If thou thinkest this an equal wish, choose wealth and length of days. Be thou mighty in the world, O Nachiketas; I make thee an enjoyer of thy desires.

Whatsoever desires are difficult in the mortal world, ask all desires according to thy will.

These beauties, with their chariots and lutes — not such as these are to be won by men — be waited on by them, my gifts. Ask me not of death, Nachiketas.

Nachiketas speaks :

To-morrow these fleeting things wear out the vigour of a mortal's powers. Even the whole of life is short; thine are chariots and dance and song.

Not by wealth can a man be satisfied. Shall we choose wealth if we have seen thee? Shall we desire life while thou art master? But the wish I choose is truly that.

Coming near to the unfading immortals, a fading mortal here below, and understanding, thinking on the sweets of beauty and pleasure, who would rejoice in length of days?

This that they doubt about, O Death, what is in the great Beyond, tell me of that. This wish that draws near to the mystery, Nachiketas chooses no other wish than that.

Death speaks:

The better is one thing, the dearer is another thing; these two bind a man in opposite ways. Of these two, it is well for him who takes the better; he fails of his object, who chooses the dearer.

The better and the dearer approach a man; going round them, the sage discerns between them. The sage chooses the better rather than the dearer; the fool chooses the dearer, through lust of possession.

Thou indeed, pondering on dear and dearly-loved desires, O Nachiketas, hast passed them by. Not this way of wealth hast thou chosen, in which many men sink.

Far apart are these two ways, un-wisdom and what is known as wisdom. I esteem Nachiketas as one seeking wisdom, nor do manifold desires allure thee.

Others, turning about in unwisdom, self-wise and thinking they are learned, fools, stagger, lagging in the way, like the blind led by the blind.

The great Beyond gleams not for the child, led away by the delusion of possessions. "This is the world, there is no other," he thinks, and so falls again and again under my dominion.

That is not to be gained even for a hearing by many, and hearing it many understand it not. Wonderful is the speaker of it, blessed the receiver; wonderful is the knower of it, taught by the blessed.

Not by the lower man is this, when declared, to be known even by much meditation. There is no way to it unless told by the other, very subtle is it, nor can it be debated by formal logic.

The understanding of this cannot be gained by debate; but it is declared by the other, dearest, for a right understanding. Thou hast obtained it, for thou art steadfast in the truth; may a questioner like thee, Nachiketas, come to us.

" I know that what they call treasure

is unenduring; and by unlasting things what is lasting cannot be obtained. Therefore the Nachiketas fire was kindled by me, and for these unenduring things I have gained that which endures."

Thus saying, and having beheld the obtaining of longings, the resting-place of the world, the endlessness of desire, the shore where there is no fear, greatly praised, and the wide-sung resting-place, thou, Nachiketas, wise in thy firmness, hast passed them by.

But that which is hard to see, which has entered the secret place, and is hidden in secret, the mystery, the ancient; understanding that bright one by the path of union with the inner self, the wise man leaves exultation and sorrow behind.

A mortal, hearing this and understanding it, drawing forth that subtle righteous one from all things else, and obtaining it, rejoices, having gained good cause for rejoicing; and the door to it is wide open, I think, Nachiketas.

Nachiketas speaks:
What thou seest to be neither the law nor lawlessness, neither what is

commanded nor what is forbidden; neither what has been nor what shall be, tell me that.

Death speaks:

That resting-place which all the Vedas proclaim, and all austerities declare; seeking for which they enter the service of the Eternal, that resting-place I briefly tell to thee.

It is the unchanging Eternal, it is the unchanging supreme; having understood that unchanging one, whatsoever a man wishes, that he gains. It is the excellent foundation, the supreme foundation; knowing that foundation, a man is mighty in the eternal world.

The knower is never born nor dies, nor is it from anywhere, nor did it become anything. Unborn, eternal, immemorial, this ancient is not slain when the body is slain.

If the slayer thinks to slay it, if the slain thinks it is slain, neither of them understand; this slays not nor is slain. Smaller than small, greater than great, this Self is hidden in the heart of man. He who has ceased from desire, and passed sorrow by, through the favour of that ordainer beholds the greatness of the Self.

Though seated, it travels far; though at rest, it goes everywhere; who but me is worthy to know this bright one who is joy without rejoicing?

Understanding this great lord the Self, bodiless in bodies, stable among unstable, the wise man cannot grieve. This Self is not to be gained by speaking of it, nor by ingenuity, nor by much hearing. Whom this chooses, by him it is gained, and the Self chooses his form as its own.

He who has ceased not from evil, who is not at peace, who stands not firm whose emotions are not at rest, cannot obtain it by knowledge.

Priest and Warrior are its food, its anointing is death; who knows truly where it is?

Death speaks:

The knowers of the Eternal, those of the five fires, and of the triple fire of Nachiketas, tell of the shadow and the fire—*the soul and the spirit*—entering into the cave and drinking their reward in the world of good works, on the higher path.

This is the bridge of the sacrificers, the undying Eternal, the supreme, the fearless, the harbour of those who would cross over—may we master the fire of Nachiketas.

Know that the Self is the lord of the chariot, the body verily is the chariot; know that the soul is the charioteer, and emotion the reins.

They say that the bodily powers are the horses, and that the external world is their field. When the Self, the bodily powers and emotion are joined together, this is the right enjoyer; thus say the wise.

But for the unwise, with emotion ever unrestrained, his bodily powers run away with him, like the unruly horses of the charioteer.

For him who is wise, with emotion ever restrained, his bodily powers do not run away with him, like the well-ruled horses of the charioteer.

But he who is unwise, restrains not emotion, and is ever impure, gains not that resting-place, but returns to the world of birth and death.

He who is wise, restrains emotion, and is ever pure, gains that resting-place from which he is not born again.

He whose charioteer is wisdom, who grasps the reins — emotion — firmly, he indeed gains the end of the path, the supreme resting-place of the emanating Power.

The impulses are higher than the bodily powers; emotion is higher than the impulses; soul is higher than emotion; higher than soul is the Self, the great one.

Higher than this great one is the unmanifest; higher than the unmanifest is spirit. Than spirit nothing is higher, for it is the goal, and the supreme way.

This is the hidden Self; in all beings it shines not forth; but is perceived by the piercing subtle soul of the subtle-sighted.

Let the wise hold formative voice and emotion; let him hold them in the Self which is wisdom; let him hold this wisdom in the Self which is great; and this let him hold in the Self which is peace.

Rise up! awake! and, having obtained your wishes, understand them.

The sages say this path is hard, difficult to tread as the keen edge of a razor.

He is released from the mouth of Death, having gained the lasting thing which is above the great, which has neither sound nor touch nor form nor change nor taste nor smell, but is eternal, beginningless, endless.

This is the immemorial teaching of Nachiketas, declared by Death. Speaking it and hearing it the sage is mighty in the eternal world. Whosoever, being pure, shall cause this supreme secret to be heard, in the assembly of those who seek the Eternal, or at the time of the union with those who have gone forth, he indeed builds for endlessness, he builds for endlessness.

IN THE HOUSE OF DEATH

THE SECOND PART

THE Self-Being pierced the openings outward; hence one looks outward, not within himself. A wise man looked towards the Self with reverted sight, seeking deathlessness.

Children seek after outward desires; they come to the net of widespread death. But the wise, beholding deathlessness, seek not for the enduring among unenduring things.

By that which perceives form, taste, smell, sounds, and embraces; by this verily he discerns, for what else is there? This is that.

The wise man, thinking that that by which he perceives both waking and dreaming life, is the great, the lord, the Self, grieves not.

He who perceives the living Self, the honey-eater, close at hand, the lord of what has been and what shall be, he is no longer seeking for refuge. This is that.

He who knows the first-born of radiance, born of old of the waters, standing hid in secret, who looked forth through creatures. This is that.

And the great mother, full of divinity, who comes forth through life, standing hid in secret, who was born through creatures. This is that.

The fire hidden in the fire sticks — like a germ, well concealed by the mothers — that fire is day by day to be praised by men who wake, with the oblation. This is that.

Whence the sun rises, and whither he goes to setting; that all the bright ones rest on, nor does any go beyond it. This is that.

What is here, that is there; what is there, that also is here. He goes from death to death who sees a difference between them.

This is to be received by the mind, that there is no difference here. From death to death he goes, who sees a difference.

The spirit of the measure of a finger stands in the midst, in the Self; lord of what has been, and what shall be. Thereafter one is no longer seeking for refuge. This is that.

The spirit of the measure of a finger is like a light without smoke; lord of what has been and what shall be, the same to-day and to-morrow. This is that.

As water rained on broken ground runs away among the mountains; so he who beholds separate natures runs hither and thither after them.

As pure water poured in pure remains the same, so is the Self of the discerning sage, O descendant of Gotama.

Understanding the eleven-doored dwelling of the unborn seer of truth, he grieves not; and, freed, he is set free. This is that.   .

This is the Swan in the pure world, the radiant in the middle world, the fire here on the altar; as a guest in a dwelling.

This is the essence of man, the essence of the best, the essence of the deep and the ether; those born of the water, of earth, of the deep, of the mountains, are that true great one.

He leads upward the forward-life, and casts back the downward-life. All the bright powers bow to the dwarf seated in their midst.

When this lord of the body, stand- ing within the body, departs; when he goes forth free from the body, what is left? This is that.

No mortal lives by the forward-life, nor by the downward-life. But by another they live, in whom these two rest.

This secret immemorial Eternal, I shall declare to thee; and how the Self is, on attaining death, O descendant of Gotama.

Some come to the womb, for the embodying of that lord of the body. Others reach the resting-place, according to deeds, according to what they have understood.

The spirit that wakes in those that dream, moulding desire after desire, is that bright one, that Eternal; that they call the immortal one. In this all the worlds rest, nor does any go beyond it. This is that.

As fire, being one, on entering the world, is assimilated to form after form; so the inner Self of all being is assimilated to form after form, and yet remains outside them.

As the air, being one, on entering the world, is assimilated to form after form; so the inner Self of all being is assimilated to form after form, and yet remains outside them.

As the sun, the eye of all the world, is not smeared by visible outer stains; so the inner Self of all being is not smirched by sorrow of the world, but remains outside it.

The one ruler, the inner Self of all being, who makes one form manifold; the wise who behold him within themselves, theirs is happiness, and not others'.

The durable among undurables; the soul of souls, who though one, disposes the desires of many; the wise who behold him within themselves, theirs is peace everlasting, and not others'.

This is that, they think, the ineffable supreme joy. How then may I know, whether this shines or borrows its light? No sun shines there, nor the moon and stars; nor lightnings, nor fire like this. All verily shines after that shining. From the shining of that, all this borrows light.

Rooted above, with branches below,

is this immemorial Tree. It is that bright one, that Eternal; it is called the immortal. In it all the worlds rest; nor does any go beyond it. This is that.

All that the universe is, moves in life, emanated from it. It is the great fear, the upraised thunderbolt. They who have seen it, become immortal.

Through fear of this, Fire glows; through fear of this, the Sun glows; through fear of it, the King and Breath; and Death runs, as fifth.

If one has been able to understand it here, before the body's falling away, he builds for embodiment in the creative worlds.

As in a mirror, this is seen in the Self; as in a dream, it is seen in the world; as in the waters around, it is seen in the world of sylphs; as in the fire and the shadow, it is seen in the world of the Evolver.

Considering the life of the powers as apart, and their rising and setting as they grow up apart, the wise man grieves not.

Mind is higher than the powers, the real is higher than mind; than this real, the great Self is higher;

and than the great, the unmanifest is higher.

Than the unmanifest, spirit is higher, the universal and formless; knowing which a being is released, and goes to immortality.

The form of this does not stand visible, nor does anyone behold it with the eye. By the heart, the soul, the mind, it is grasped; and those who know it become immortal.

When the five perceptions and mind are steadied; and when the soul struggles not, this, they say, is the highest way.

This they think to be union, the firm holding of the powers. Unperturbed is this union, though there be ebb and flow.

Nor by speech, nor by mind can it be gained; nor by sight. It is gained by him who can affirm "It is"; how else could it be gained?

It is to be gained by affirming "It is"; and as the real in what is and is not. In him who obtains it by affirming "It is" its reality is perfected.

When all desires that dwell in his heart are let go, the mortal becomes immortal, and reaches the Eternal.

When all the knots of his heart In the are untied here, the mortal becomes House of immortal.   So far is the teaching. Death

A hundred and one are the heart's channels; of these one passes to the crown. Going up by this, he comes to the immortal.   The others lead hither and thither.

The spirit of the measure of a finger, the inner Self, ever dwells in the hearts of men. Let him draw forth this spirit from his body, firmly, like the pith from a reed.

Let him know that this is the bright one, the immortal. Let him know it is the bright one, the immortal.

Nachiketas thus having received the knowledge declared by Death, and the whole law of union, became a passionless dweller in the Eternal, and deathless; and so may another who thus knows the union with the Self.

II

A VEDIC MASTER

HESE men, Sukeshan Bhâr-advâja, and Shâivya Saty-akâma, and Sâuryâyanin Gârgya, and Kâushalya Ashvalâyana, and Bhârgava Vâidarbhi, and Kabandhin Kâtyâyana, full of the Eternal, firm in the Eternal, were seeking after the supreme Eternal.

They came to the Master Pippalâda, with fuel in their hands, saying: He verily will declare it all.

And the Sage said to them: Remain yet a year in fervour, service of the Eternal, and faith. Ask whatever questions you will, if we know them, we shall declare all to you.

So Kabandhin Kâtyâyana, approaching, asked: Master, where are all these beings brought forth from?

He answered him: The Lord of beings desired beings. He brooded with fervour; and, brooding with fervour, he forms a Pair. They are the Substance and the Life. These two will make beings manifold for me, said he. The sun verily is the

Life, and Substance is the moon. For Substance is all that is formed, and the formless *is the Life.* Therefore the form is the Substance.

So the sun, rising, enters the eastern space; and thus he gathers all the eastern lives among his rays. As the southern, the western, the northern, the nether, and the upper space, and the spaces between, as he illumines all, so he gathers all lives among his rays. Thus the Life rises as universal, all-formed fire.

And this is declared by the Vedic verse:

> The all-formed, golden Illuminer, the supreme way, the light, the fervent one. Thousand-rayed, turning in a hundred ways, the Life of beings, this sun rises.

The year is a Lord of beings. His two paths are the southern and the northern. Therefore they who worship, thinking that it is fulfilled by sacrifice and gifts, win the lunar world. They verily return again. Therefore these sages who desire beings, turn to the south. For this is the path of Substance, the path of the fathers.

But they who by the northern way seek the Self by fervour, service of the Eternal, faith and knowledge, they verily win the sun. This is the home of lives; this is the immortal, fearless, supreme way. From it they do not return again; for this is the end.

And there is this verse:

They call *the sun* the father in the
upper half of heaven, with five
steps—*seasons*—and twelve forms
—*months*—the giver of increase.

But others call him the Seer who
rests in the seven-wheeled chariot,
of six spokes.

The month is a Lord of beings. The dark half is the Substance; the bright half is the Life. Therefore these Sages offer sacrifice in the bright half; but the others in the other half.

Day-and-night is a Lord of beings. Day verily is the Life, and night is the Substance. They waste their life who find love in the outward; but service of the Eternal finds love in the hidden.

Food also is a Lord of beings. Thence comes this seed, and thence these beings are brought forth. And all that follow this vow of the Lord of beings, produce a pair.

Theirs verily is that world of the Eternal, who have fervour and service of the Eternal, and in whom truth is set firm. Theirs is that quiet world of the Eternal; but not theirs, in whom are crookedness, untruth, illusion.

And so Bhârgava Vâidarbhi asked him: Master, how many are the bright ones that uphold being? Which illumine this? Which of them again is chiefest?

He answered him: Shining ether is that bright one, air, and fire, and water, and earth; voice, mind, sight, hearing. They, illumining, declare: We uphold this ray, establishing it.

And Life, the chiefest among them, said: Cherish not this delusion: for I, verily, dividing myself fivefold, uphold this ray, establishing it.

They were incredulous. Life proudly made as if to go out above. And as Life goes out, all the others go out, and as Life returns, all the others return. As the bees all go out after the honey-makers' king when he goes out, and return when he returns, thus did voice, mind, sight, and hearing. Joyful, they sing the praise of Life.

He warms as fire; as sun, and the rain-god; the thunderer, wind, and the earth, substance, the bright one; what is, what is not, and what is immortal.

Like spokes in a wheel's nave, all this rests in Life. Songs, and liturgies, and chants; sacrifice and warrior and priest.

Thou, Life, as Lord of beings, movest in the germ; and thou thyself art born from it. And to thee, Life, these beings bring the offering; thou who art set firm through the lives.

Thou art the tongued flame of the bright ones; the first oblation of the fathers. Thou art the law of the sages; the truth of sacrificial priests.

Thou art the thunderer, Life, with his brightness; thou art the storm-god, the preserver. Thou movest in the mid space as the sun; thou art master of the stars.

When thou descendest as rain, these thy children, Life, stand rejoicing; we shall have food, they say, according to our desire.

Thou art the exile, Life, the lonely seer; the eater, the good master of all. We are givers of the first offering. Thou art father to us, the great Breath.

Thy form that is manifested in voice, and in hearing, and in sight, and the form that expands in mind, make it auspicious! Go not out!

All this is in Life's sway, all that is set firm in the triple heaven. Guard us as a mother her sons; and as Fortune, give us wisdom!

And so Kâushalya Ashvalâyana asked him: Master, where is this Life born from? How does it enter this body? How does it come forth, dividing itself? Through what does it go out? How does it envelop the outer? and how as to union with the Self?

He answered him: Many questions thou askest! Thou art full of the Eternal, and therefore I tell it to thee.

From the Self is this Life born. And as the shadow beside a man, this is expanded in that. By mind's action it enters this body. And as a sovereign commands his lords: These villages and these villages shall ye rule over! Thus also Life disposes the lesser lives. For the lower powers, the downward-life; in sight and hearing, in mouth and nose, the forward-life; and in the midst, the binding-life; this binds together the food that is offered; and thence the seven flames arise.

In the heart is the Self. Here are a hundred and one channels. From them a hundred each, and in each of these, two and seventy thousand branch-channels. In these the distributing-life moves.

And by one, the upward, rises the upward-life. It leads by holiness to a holy world, by sin to a sinful world, by both, to the world of men.

The outward-life rises as the sun. It is linked with this life that dwells in seeing. And the potency that is in earth, entering the downward-life of man, establishes it. And the shining ether is for the binding-life, and air for the distributing-life.

And radiance for the upward-life.

Therefore he whose radiance has become quiescent is reborn through the impulses dwelling in mind. According to his thoughts, he enters life. And Life joined by the radiance with the Self leads him to a world according to his will.

He who, thus knowing, knows Life, his being fails not, and he becomes immortal.

And there is this verse:

Knowing the source, the range, the abode, the lordship of Life fivefold, and its union with the Self, he reaches immortality, he reaches immortality.

And so Sâuryâyanin Gârgya asked him: Master, how many powers sleep in the man? How many wake in him? Who is the bright one that sees dreams? Whose is that bliss? and in whom are all these set firm?

He answered him: As, Gârgya, the rays of the sun, at setting, all become one in his shining orb; and when he rises, they all come forth again; so all becomes one in the higher bright one, mind.

Therefore the man hears not, nor sees nor smells, nor tastes, nor touches, nor speaks, nor takes, nor enjoys, nor puts forth, nor moves. He sleeps, they say.

The life-fires verily wake in this dwelling. The household fire is the downward-life. The fire of oblations is the distributing-life. And as the fire of offerings is brought forward from the household fire, it is the forward-life.

And the binding-life is what binds together the offerings, the outbreathing and inbreathing. Mind is the sacrificer, and the upward-life is the fruit of the sacrifice. For it brings the sacrificer day by day to the Eternal.

So this bright one in dream enjoys greatness. The seen, as seen he beholds again. What was heard, as heard he hears again. And what was enjoyed by the other powers, he enjoys again by the other powers. The seen and the unseen, heard and unheard, enjoyed and unenjoyed, real and unreal, he sees it all; as All he sees it.

And when he is wrapt by the radiance, the bright one no longer sees dreams. Then within him that bliss arises. And, dear, as the birds come to the tree to rest, so all this comes to rest in the higher Self.

Earth and earth-forms; water and water-forms; light and light-forms; air and air-forms; ether and ether-forms; seeing and seen; hearing and heard; smelling and smelled; taste and tasted; touch and touched; voice and spoken; hands and handled; feet and moving; mind and minding; knowledge and knowing; personality and personal; imagination and imagining; radiance and enlightening; life and living.

For this Self is the seer, toucher, hearer, smeller, taster, thinker, knower, doer, the perceiving spirit. And this is set firm in the supreme, unchanging Self.

He reaches the supreme unchanging who knows that shadowless, bodiless, colourless, bright unchanging one. He, dear, becomes all-knowing, becomes the All.

And there is this verse:

He who knows the unchanging one
    where are set firm the perceiving
    self, with all the powers, all lives

and beings; he, verily, all-know-

And so Shâivya Satyakâma asked him: And he amongst men, Master, who to the end of his life meditates on the mystic Om; what world will he gain by it?

And he answered him: This mystic Om, Satyakâma, is for the higher and lower Eternal. Therefore the wise man, by dwelling on this, reaches one of these: if he meditates on the first measure, enlightened by it he is quickly reborn in the world. The songs bring him to the world of men; there, full of fervour, service of the Eternal, and faith, he enjoys greatness.

And if he dwells on it in his mind with two measures, he is led to the middle world by the liturgies. He wins the lunar world, and after enjoying brightness in the lunar world, he returns again.

And he who with three measures meditates on the mystic Om, and thereby meditates on the supreme spirit, is endowed with radiance, with the sun; as a serpent is freed from its slough, he is, verily, freed from sin.

He is led by the chants to the world of the Eternal. He beholds the indwelling spirit above the highest assemblage of lives.

And there are these two verses:

The three measures are subject to death when divided; they are joined to each other, but not inseparable. When the outer, the middle, and the midmost forms are joined together, the knower is not shaken.

By the songs to this world; by the liturgies to the middle world; by the chants to the world the seers tell of; by meditating on the mystic Om, the wise man reaches that peace, unfading, immortal, fearless, supreme.

And so Sukeshan Bhâradvâja asked him: Master, the Râjaputra, Hiranyanâbha Kâusalya, coming to me, asked this question: Bhâradvâja, knowest thou the spirit with sixteen parts? I answered the youth: I know him not; if I knew him, how should I not tell thee? He withers, root and all, who speaks untruth; therefore I deign not to speak untruth. He, silently, entering his chariot, departed. I ask thee where this spirit is.

He answered him: Here, verily, within the body, dear, is that spirit in which the sixteen parts come forth.

He said: In whose going out shall I go out? In whose resting shall I rest firm? He put forth Life; and, from Life, faith, the shining ether, air, light, the waters, and the power of earth. Then mind and food, and, from food, force and fervour, the hymns, the words of action, and name in the worlds.

And as these rivers, rolling oceanwards, go to their setting on reaching the ocean, and their name and form are lost in the ocean, they say. So the sixteen parts of this seer, moving spiritwards, on reaching spirit, go to their setting; their name and form are lost in spirit, they say. He becomes one, without parts, and immortal.

And there is this verse:

In whom the parts are fixed like the spokes in the nave of a wheel; knowing that knowable spirit, let not death disturb you.

He said to them: So far I know

that supreme Eternal. There is
nothing beyond.

Thou art our father, inasmuch as
thou hast made us cross over to the
further shore of unwisdom, said they,
honouring him.

III

THAT THOU ART

HERE lived once Shvetaketu, Aruna's grandson; his father addressed him, saying:

Shvetaketu, go, learn the service of the Eternal; for no one, dear, of our family is an unlearned nominal worshipper.

So going when he was twelve years old, he returned when he was twenty-four; he had learned all the teachings, but was conceited, vain of his learning, and proud.

His father addressed him:

Shvetaketu, you are conceited, vain of your learning, and proud, dear; but have you asked for that teaching through which the unheard is heard, the unthought is thought, the unknown is known?

What sort of teaching is that, Master? said he.

Just as, dear, by a single piece of clay anything made of clay may be known, for the difference is only one of words and names, and the real thing is that it is of clay; or just as, dear, by one jewel of gold, anything made of gold may be known, for the difference is only one of words and names, and the real is that it is gold; or just as, dear, by a single knife-blade, anything made of iron may be known, for the difference is only one of words and names, and the real is that it is iron; just like this is the teaching that makes the unknown known.

But I am sure that those teachers did not know this themselves; for if they had known it, how would they not have taught it to me? said he; but now let my Master tell it to me.

Let it be so, dear; said he.

In the beginning, dear, there was Being, alone and secondless. But there are some who say that there was non-Being in the beginning, alone and secondless; so that Being would be born from non-Being; but how could this be so, dear? said he; how could Being be born from non-Being? So there was Being, dear, in the beginning, alone and secondless.

Then Being beholding said: Let
me become great; let me give birth.

Then it put forth Radiance.

Then Radiance beholding said: Let
me become great; let me give birth.

Then it put forth the Waters. Just
as a man is hot and sweats, so from
radiance the waters are born.

Then the Waters beholding said:
Let us become great; let us give
birth.

They put forth the world-food.
Just as when it rains much food is
produced, so from the Waters the
world-food — *Earth* — is born.

Of all these, of beings, there are
three germs: what is born of the Egg,
what is born of Life, what is born of
Division.

That power — *Being* — beholding
said: Let me enter these three
powers — *Radiance, Waters, Earth* —
by this life, by my Self, let me give
them manifold forms and names.
Let me make each one of them threefold, threefold.

So that power — *Being* — entered
those three powers — *Radiance, Waters, Earth* — by this life, by the Self,

and gave them manifold forms and names; and so made each one of them threefold, threefold. And now learn, dear, how these three powers are, how each one of them becomes threefold, threefold.

In fire, the radiant form is from Radiance; the clear form, from the Waters; the dark form, from Earth. But the separate nature of fire is a thing of names and words only, while the real thing is the three forms.

So of the sun, the radiant form is from Radiance; the clear form, from the Waters; the dark form, from Earth. But the separate nature of the sun is a thing of names and words only, while the real thing is the three forms.

So of the moon, the radiant form is from Radiance; the clear form, from the Waters; the dark form, from Earth. But the separate nature of the moon is a thing of names and words only, while the real thing is the three forms.

So of lightning, the radiant form is from Radiance; the clear form, from the Waters; the dark form, from

Earth. But the separate nature of lightning is a thing of names and words only, the real thing is the three forms.

Therefore of old time those who knew this, the great sages and teachers of old, spoke thus: None of us may now speak of anything as unheard, unthought, unknown.

For by these three forms they knew everything. For whatever was like radiant, its form was from Radiance, they said, and thus knew it. And whatever was like clear, its form was from the Waters, they said, and so knew it. And whatever was like dark, its form was from Earth, they said, and so knew it. Thus whatever was known they took to be a union of these three powers, and thus they knew it.

But how these three powers are, dear, when they come to man, how each of them becomes threefold, this learn from me now.

Food that is eaten is divided threefold. Its grossest part becomes waste; its middle part becomes flesh; its lightest part becomes Mind.

Waters that are drunk are divided threefold. The grossest part becomes waste; the middle part becomes blood; the lightest part becomes vital Breath.

Things that produce radiant heat, when absorbed, are divided threefold. The grossest part becomes bone; the middle part becomes nerve; the lightest part becomes formative Voice.

For Mind, dear, is formed of the world-food — *Earth*; vital Breath is formed of the Waters; formative Voice is formed of Radiance.

Let my master teach me further; said he.

Be it so, dear; said he.

Of churned milk, dear, the lightest part rises to the top and becomes butter. Just so of eaten food, dear, the lightest part rises to the top and becomes Mind. And so of waters that are drunk, the lightest part rises to the top, and becomes vital Breath. And so when heat-giving things are eaten, the lightest part rises to the top, and becomes formative Voice.

For Mind, dear, is formed of Food;

vital Breath is formed of the Waters; That
formative Voice is formed of Radiance. Thou
Art

Let my Master teach me further;
said he.

Be it so, dear; said he.

Man, dear, is made of sixteen parts.
Eat nothing for fifteen days, but drink
as much as you wish; for vital Breath,
being formed of the Waters, is cut off
if you do not drink.

He ate nothing for fifteen days, and
then returned to the Master, saying:
What shall I repeat, Master?

Repeat the songs and liturgies and
chants, dear; said he.

None of them come back into my
mind, Master; said he.

He said to him: As, dear, after a
big fire, if a single spark remain, as
big as a fire-fly, it will not burn much;
just so, dear, of your sixteen parts one
remains, and by this one part you
cannot remember the teachings.

Go, eat; and then you will understand me.

He ate, and then returned to the
Master; and whatever the Master
asked, all came back to his mind.

The Master said to him: As, dear,
after a big fire, if even a single spark
remain, as big as a fire-fly, and if it be
fed with straw, it will blaze up and
will then burn much; just so, dear, of
your sixteen parts, one part was left;
and this, being fed with food, blazed
up, and through it you remembered
the teachings.

For Mind is formed of Food; vital
Breath is formed of the Waters; formative Voice is formed of Radiance.

Thus he learned; thus, verily, he
learned.

RUNA's son Uddâlaka ad-
dressed his son Shvetaketu,
saying: Learn from me,
dear, the reality about sleep. When
a man sinks to sleep, as they say,
then, dear, he is wrapped by the Real;
he has slipped back to his own. And
so they say he sleeps, because he has
slipped back to his own. And just as
an eagle tied by a cord, flying hither
and thither, and finding no other
resting place, comes to rest where he
is tied, so indeed, dear, the man's
Mind flying hither and thither, and

finding no other resting place, comes to rest in vital Breath; for Mind, dear, is bound by vital Breath.

Learn from me, dear, the meaning of hunger and thirst. When a man hungers, as they say, the Waters guide what he eats. And as there are guides of cows, guides of horses, guides of men, so they call the Waters the guides of what is eaten. Thus you must know, dear, that what he eats grows and sprouts forth; and it cannot grow without a root.

And where can the root of what he eats be? Where, but in the world-food — *Earth*?

And through the world-food — *Earth* — that has sprouted forth, you must seek the root, the Waters. And through the waters that have sprouted forth, you must seek the root, Radiance. And through Radiance that has sprouted forth, you must seek the root, the Real. For all these beings, dear, are rooted in the Real, resting in the Real, abiding in the Real.

And so when the man thirsts, as they say, the Radiance guides what he drinks. And as there are guides of cows, guides of horses, guides of men, so, they say, the Radiance guides the Waters. Thus you must know, dear, that what he drinks grows and sprouts forth; and it cannot grow without a root.

And where can the root of what he drinks be? Where, but in the Waters? And through the Waters that sprout forth, you must seek their root, the Radiance. And through the Radiance, dear, that sprouts forth, you must seek its root, the Real. For all these beings, dear, are rooted in the Real, resting in the Real, abiding in the Real. And how these three: the world-food — *Earth* — the Waters, Radiance, coming to a man, become each threefold, threefold, this has been taught already.

And of a man who goes forth, formative Voice sinks back into Mind; Mind sinks back into vital Breath, vital Breath to Radiance, and Radiance to the higher Divinity. This is the soul, the Self of all that is, this is the Real, this the Self, THAT THOU ART, O Shvetaketu.

Let the Master teach me more; said he.

Let it be so, dear; said he.

As the honey-makers, dear, gather the honey from many a tree, and weld the nectars together in a single nectar; and as they find no separateness there, nor say: Of that tree I am the nectar, of that tree I am the nectar. Thus, indeed, dear, all these beings, when they reach the Real, know not, nor say: We have reached the Real. But whatever they are here, whether tiger or lion or wolf or boar or worm or moth or gnat or fly, that they become again. And this soul is the Self of all that is, this is the Real, this the Self. THAT THOU ART, O Shvetaketu.

Let the Master teach me more; said he.

Let it be so, dear; said he.

These eastern rivers, dear, roll eastward; and the western, westward. From the ocean to the ocean they go, and in the ocean they are united. And there they know no separateness, nor say: This am I, this am I. Thus indeed, dear, all these beings, coming forth from the Real, know not, nor say: We have come from the Real.

And whatever they are here, whether tiger or lion or wolf or boar or worm or moth or gnat or fly or whatever they are, that they become again. And that soul is the Self of all that is, this is the Real, this the Self. THAT THOU ART, O Shvetaketu.

Let the Master teach me more; said he.

Let it be so, dear; said he.

If any one strike the root of this great tree, dear, it will flow and live, if any one strike the middle of it, it will flow and live; if any one strike the top of it, it will flow and live. So filled with Life, with the Self, drinking in and rejoicing, it stands firm. But if the life of it leaves one branch, that branch dries up; it leaves a second, that dries up; it leaves a third, that dries up; it leaves the whole, the whole dries up. Thus indeed, dear, you must understand; said he. When abandoned by Life, verily, this dies; but Life itself does not die. For that soul is the Self of all that is, this is the Real, this the Self. THAT THOU ART, O Shvetaketu.

Let the Master teach me more;
said he.

That Thou Art

Let it be so, dear; said he.

Bring me a fruit of that fig-tree.

Here is the fruit, Master.

Divide it into two; said he.

I have divided it, Master.

What do you see in it? said he.

Atom-like seeds, Master.

Divide one of them in two; said he.

I have divided it, Master.

What do you see in it? said he.

I see nothing at all, Master.

So he said to him:

That soul that you perceive not at all, dear,—from that very soul the great fig-tree comes forth. Believe then, dear, that this soul is the Self of all that is, this is the Real, this the Self. THAT THOU ART, O Shvetaketu.

Let the Master teach me more; said he.

Let it be so, dear; said he.

Put this salt in water, and come to me early in the morning.

And he did so, and the Master said to him:

57

That salt you put in the water last night — bring it to me! And looking for its appearance, he could not see it, as it was melted in the water.

Taste the top of it; said he. How is it?

It is salt; said he.

Taste the middle of it; said he. How is it?

It is salt; said he.

Taste the bottom of it; said he. How is it?

It is salt; said he.

Take it away, then, and return to me.

And he did so; but that exists for ever. And the master said to him:

Just so, dear, you do not see the Real in the world. Yet it is here all the same. And this soul is the Self of all that is, this is the Real, this the Self. THAT THOU ART, O Shvetaketu.

Let the Master teach me more; said he.

Let it be so, dear; said he.

Just as if they were to blindfold a man, and lead him far away from Gandhâra, and leave him in the wilderness; and as he cried to the east and the north and the west: I am led away blindfolded; I am deserted blindfolded. And just as if one came, and loosing the bandage from his eyes, told him: In that direction is Gandhâra; in that direction you must go. And he asking from village to village like a wise man and learned, should come safe to Gandhâra. Thus, verily, a man who has found the true Teacher, knows. He must wait only till he is free, then he reaches the resting-place. And that soul is the Self of all that is, this is the Real, this the Self. THAT THOU ART, O Shvetaketu.

Let the Master teach me more; said he.

Let it be so, dear; said he.

When a man is near his end, his friends gather round him: Do you know me, do you know me? they say. And until formative Voice sinks back into Mind, and Mind into Breath, and Breath into the Radiance, and the Radiance into the higher Divinity, he still knows them. But when formative Voice sinks back into Mind, and Mind into Breath, and Breath into the Radiance, and the Radiance into the higher Divinity, he knows them not. And that soul is the Self of all that is, this is the Real, this the Self. THAT THOU ART, O Shvetaketu.

Let the Master-teach me more; said he.

Let it be so, dear; said he.

They bind a man and bring him: He has stolen, they say; he has committed theft. Heat the axe *for the ordeal:* and if he is the doer of it, and makes himself untrue; maintaining untruth, and wrapping himself in untruth, he grasps the heated axe; he burns, and so dies. But if he be not the doer of it, he makes himself true; maintaining truth, and wrapping himself in truth, he grasps the heated axe; he burns not, and so goes free. And the truth that saves him from burning is the Self of all that is, this is the Real, this the Self. THAT THOU ART, O Shvetaketu.

Thus he learned the truth; thus he learned it.

FOUR HUNDRED AND FIFTY
COPIES OF THIS BOOK (SEC-
OND EDITION) HAVE BEEN
PRINTED ON VAN GELDER
HAND-MADE PAPER, AND
TYPE DISTRIBUTED, IN THE
MONTH OF SEPTEMBER, A. D.
MDCCCXCIX, AT THE PRESS OF
SMITH & SALE, PORTLAND,
MAINE.